Kathryn White

has written over two dozen
children's books. When she is not
writing, Kathryn visits schools and
libraries telling stories and leading
activities. She lives in England with
her husband and children.

Miriam Latimer

studied illustration at the University
of the West of England. She now works as
a full-time illustrator and combines this
with workshops for primary school children.
Miriam lives with her husband in England.
Ruby's Sleepover is her sixth project
with Barefoot Books.

Ruby's Sleepover

Written by **Kathryn White**

Illustrated by **Miriam Latimer**

Barefoot Books
step inside a story

I'm sleeping with Mai in my tent tonight,
When the **moon** is full and the **stars** are bright.

We're both so excited!
We **whoop** and we **jump**,
Into the tent we **tumble** and **bump**.

One bag on this side, one bag on that,
Mai's brought her teddy,
and I've brought my cat.

I open my backpack and show Mai my things:
My **egg**
and my **beans**
and my **magical rings**.

We nibble our snacks,
and hear foxes bark.
Then turn on our flashlights
to see in the **dark**.

The **moon** shines above us;

there's no one about.

We snuggle down deep

with our eyes peeking out.

I'm not at all nervous; I feel quite prepared.

"Don't worry," I say,

"there's no need to be scared."

But a **rumble** —

a **grumble!** —

roars loud down the street.

Mai grabs my arm and jumps to her feet.

I giggle and say, "A **giant** is near."

Mai screeches out,

"Don't let it in here!"

"I'll toss out these **beans**

so they'll grow up so high

That the **giant** can climb

to his home in the sky."

I hold out the beans and I give them a **shake**.

As the giant gets nearer I feel the earth **quake**.

So I open the tent flap

and throw the beans out.

"Go back to your castle,

this minute!" I shout.

An owl **hoots** a warning from high in the trees.
The tent starts to **rustle** and **shake** in the breeze.

"Did you see that shadow?"
Mai trembles in fright.
I whisper, "A **dragon** is
coming tonight."

"And when it comes **huffing**
and **puffing** about,

Snorting out
flames from its
long purple snout,

I'll send it away on a **magical quest**:
It must carry this **egg** safely back to its nest."

So I open the tent flap and call to the sky,

"Here is your **dragon's egg**, take it and fly."

I take out my **ringS** to keep danger at bay;

I slip one on my finger and give one to Mai.

We can't hear a sound now, not even a peep.

But we feel really brave as the world falls asleep.

Then Mai starts a story
her grandfather told,
Of swashbuckling **pirates**
all hunting for **gold**

With **magical ships** that sail from the **moon**.

I look up and say, "They'll be flying here soon."

"And they'll carry us off to scrub the decks clean.
They'll be **rotten** and **smelly**
and **nasty** and **mean**.

They're close to the tent now;
they're creeping around."
"**Shhh!**" I tell Mai,
"We must **not** make a sound."

But Mai is asleep,

with a sweet little **snore**.

And I really don't feel quite

as brave as before.

Then **whoosh** goes the tent flap —

My heart gives a leap.

"Wake up, Mai, I need you!"

But Mai's fast asleep.

So I hold out my **ring**

and I scrunch up my eyes,

"Oh wind, take those **pirates**

back up to the skies.

This **magical ring** will not let you near."

And I point really hard and I say,

"Disappear!"

The tent flap stops moving —

I hug my ring tight.

So **giants**

and **dragons**

and **pirates**,

"Goodnight!"

Barefoot Books
step inside a story

At Barefoot Books, we celebrate art and story that opens the hearts and minds of children from all walks of life, focusing on themes that encourage independence of spirit, enthusiasm for learning and respect for the world's diversity. The welfare of our children is dependent on the welfare of the planet, so we source paper from sustainably managed forests and constantly strive to reduce our environmental impact. Playful, beautiful and created to last a lifetime, our products combine the best of the present with the best of the past to educate our children as the caretakers of tomorrow.

www.barefootbooks.com

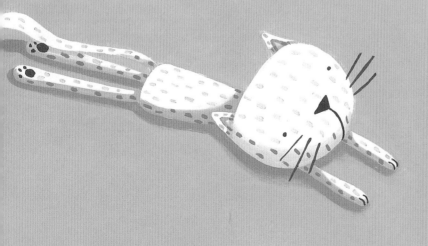